THE 12 BIGGEST BREAKTHROUGHS IN
COMMUNICATION TECHNOLOGY

by Vicki C. Hayes

12 STORY LIBRARY

www.12StoryLibrary.com

Copyright © 2019 by 12-Story Library, Mankato, MN 56003. All rights reserved. No part of this book may be reproduced or utilized in any form or by any means without written permission from the publisher.

12-Story Library is an imprint of Bookstaves.

Photographs ©: logoboom/Shutterstock.com, cover, 1; Edward Blake/CC2.0, 4; CM/Associated Press, 5; Eric Risberg/Associated Press, 6; Yuri_Arcurs/iStockphoto, 7; CTR Photos/Shutterstock.com, 8; CTRPhotos/iStockphoto, 9; AnthonyRosenberg/iStockphoto, 10; Mika1h/CC3.0, 11; ArcadeImages/Alamy Stock Photo, 12; Atari, Inc., 12; OlegDoroshin/Shutterstock.com, 13; picturesbyrob/Alamy Stock Photo, 14; BagoGames/CC2.0, 15; Jamaway/Alamy Stock Photo, 16; Iryna Tiumentseva/Shutterstock.com, 17; Zhenikeyev/iStockphoto, 18; Spencer_Whalen/iStockphoto, 19; LightFieldStudios/iStockphoto, 20; PD, 21; Wachiwit/iStockphoto, 22; dennizn/Shutterstock.com, 23; RyanKing999/iStockphoto, 24; MSSA/Shutterstock.com, 24; Mano Kors/Shutterstock.com, 25; Gorodenkoff/Shutterstock.com, 26; marcello farina/Shutterstock.com, 27; Tinxi/Shutterstock.com, 28; scyther5/iStockphoto, 29

ISBN
978-1-63235-581-2 (hardcover)
978-1-63235-635-2 (paperback)
978-1-63235-695-6 (hosted ebook)

Library of Congress Control Number: 2018937979

Printed in the United States of America
Mankato, MN
June 2018

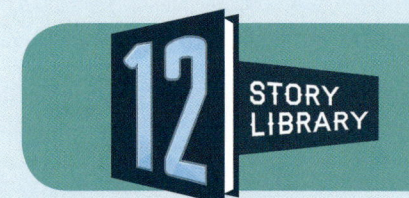

Access free, up-to-date content on this topic plus a full digital version of this book. Scan the QR code on page 31 or use your school's login at 12StoryLibrary.com.

Table of Contents

The Printing Press Spreads Knowledge and Ideas 4

Telegraph Cables Carry Dots and Dashes Around the World ... 6

Telephones Get People Talking 8

Radio Reaches Almost Everyone 10

Television Fuses Pictures and Sound 12

The Internet Connects Everything 14

Software Makes Everyone a Publisher 16

Cell Phones Let People Talk to Anyone, Anywhere 18

Email and IMing Speed Up Communication 20

Web Browsers Are Gateways to the Internet 22

Social Networking Helps People Stay Connected 24

Smartphones Put the World in Our Hands 26

Fact Sheet 28

Glossary 30

For More Information 31

Index 32

About the Author 32

The Printing Press Spreads Knowledge and Ideas

People need and like to communicate with each other. Over the years, this has led to many amazing inventions. One of the first was the printing press.

Before the middle of the 1400s, there was no mechanical printing. Everything was done by hand. It took a long time to make a book. There weren't many books. And the books that did exist were very expensive. At first, that didn't matter much. Very few people could read. In 1450, only about seven percent of people in Germany could read. But the printing press changed all that.

The first person to successfully use a printing press was Johannes Gutenberg. He was a stonecutter and goldsmith in

Gutenberg examines the first sheets printed on his press.

Germany. With his printing press, books could be made quickly. Soon more printing presses were built. By 1500, 2,500 cities in Europe had printing presses.

Ten million books had been printed. These books were cheaper than early books. Information became easier to share. New ideas were spreading quickly. More people learned how to read. Today 83 percent of all people in the world can read.

200
Number of Bibles printed by Johannes Gutenberg in 1452.

- Early books were made by hand.
- Very few people could read.
- The printing press made books quickly.
- More people learned to read.

MOVABLE METAL TYPE

The first printing presses used movable type. Each letter of the alphabet was cast in metal and attached to a block of metal or wood. The blocks were put together to make words. Lines of words made a page. First a printer would put together a whole page. Then many copies of the page could be printed quickly.

5

2

Telegraph Cables Carry Dots and Dashes Around the World

In 1830, Joseph Henry became the first person to send an electric current over a wire. The signal traveled one mile and caused a bell to strike. This invention became known as the telegraph. Wires were run between cities. The telegraph sent signals over these wires. The signals were in the form of a code. Operators translated the code. The first message was sent in 1844. It came from Washington, DC. It said Henry Clay had been nominated for president.

By 1854, the United States had 20,000 miles (32,000 km) of telegraph cable. In 1866, a line was laid across the Atlantic Ocean. It went from Ireland to Canada. Before long, there were telegraph lines from Hawaii to Asia and Australia.

Soon telegraph messages were sent and received by machines. Operators weren't needed. This meant messages went faster. In 1913, it became possible to send eight messages at once. Then 72 messages could be sent at the same time. By 1959, users could send printed documents to each other.

Today the telegraph is no longer used. But it was the first step in a long line of communication inventions.

Portrait of Joseph Henry in 1860.

Early telegraph machines required an operator.

MORSE CODE

Samuel F. B. Morse improved the telegraph and also invented the code system it used. The code used dots and dashes, which stood for letters of the alphabet. Common letters had short signals. E was one dot. Less common letters had long signals. B was dash, dot, dot, dot. The first message sent on the telegraph was from the Bible. It said, "What hath God wrought?"

40–50
Number of words a trained Morse code operator could send in one minute.

- The telegraph sent signals electronically over wires.
- The signals were in code.
- Wires were run all over the world.
- Machines replaced operators, and messages went faster.

Telephones Get People Talking

In 1876, Alexander Graham Bell was working at a school for the deaf. He was using electricity to help deaf people speak. He was also trying to improve the telegraph. He accidently invented a way to make the telephone possible. Other people were also working on the telephone. Elisha Gray applied for a telephone patent a month before Bell. But the United States Patent Office gave the patent to Bell.

The telephone allowed voices to be sent electronically over wires. To reach someone, callers would pick up a handset. Then they would dial numbers on a rotary dial. People could have conversations in real time. One of the first people to have a telephone was the author Mark Twain. Bell did not have a telephone. He thought it would distract him from his work.

In 1915, the first call was made across the United States. The first call across the Atlantic Ocean was made in 1956. The telephone saved time and money. It opened up the world. Today the telephone is an essential part of our lives. We can't imagine living without it.

Bell's first device from 1876 that could transmit speech.

SWITCHBOARD OPERATORS

The early telephone system used switchboard operators. They connected callers. They looked up telephone numbers. They answered questions. Most of these workers were women. In small towns, operators often got to know all of their customers. In big cities, operators were very busy. They couldn't take their eyes off their switchboards.

1876
Year of the first telephone call. The date was March 10.

- The telephone sent voices electronically over wires.
- Alexander Graham Bell got the first patent.
- People could talk directly to other people.
- Today telephones are essential.

4

Radio Reaches Almost Everyone

In 1895, Italian inventor Guglielmo Marconi sent the first radio signal. Radio is electronic communication through the air. It meant people could communicate over long distances without laying miles of wires. In fact, radio was first called wireless telegraphy.

In the beginning, radio sent messages using Morse code. The first radio signal sent across the Atlantic Ocean was the letter S. Sending speech wasn't possible for a few years. But in 1915, speech was sent across the United States from New York to San Francisco. It was also sent from the United States to Paris, France. For a while, radio was only used for messages. Then in 1920, the first radio station went on the air.

Marconi with his early radio apparatus.

Early radio signals were weak, so earphones were necessary to listen to radio stations.

On early radio programs, people told jokes, read bedtime stories, and read aloud from newspapers. Then radio companies built networks of stations. They started looking for shows to fill the airwaves. Soon there were many different types of programs. People listened to music and talk, comedy and drama. They heard news and information. Radio stars were born. These included Jack Benny, Burns and Allen, Abbott and Costello, Milton Berle, and Edgar Bergen.

Radio had a huge influence on American culture. Radio could reach just about everybody. It brought people from different classes and backgrounds together. Americans began to have a nationwide experience of the world.

15,500
Approximate number of radio stations in the United States as of December 31, 2017.

- Radio didn't need wires to send messages.
- Soon radio stations went on the air.
- Different types of programs were made.
- Radio had a big influence on American culture.

5 Television Fuses Pictures and Sound

People enjoyed hearing actors on the radio. But they couldn't see them. For that, they had to go to the movies. In 1928, the technology to send sound and pictures through the air was invented. This was called television. TV sets contained big glass tubes. These were called cathode ray tubes. A stream of

2,000
Approximate number of television sets in the United States before 1941.

- Television sent sound and pictures through the air.
- Many radio shows became TV shows.
- In 10 years, the number of TV sets in the United States grew from 2,000 to six million.
- Television brought people closer together.

A family watching TV in 1958.

electrons was shot from the back of the tube to the front. The electrons changed the coating on the front and images appeared.

At first, television spread slowly. The world was focused on fighting World War II. But after the war, sales of TV sets took off. So did programming. In 1941, the first black-and-white television shows were broadcast. Many favorite radio shows became television shows. By the end of 1950, there were six million TV sets in the United States. Color broadcasts began in 1951. Today 99 percent of American households have at least one TV.

Television made the world shrink. It was possible for everyone to share in the same experiences. People could see their leaders debate. They could watch their athletes compete in the Olympics. They could see news events from around the world. Television brought people closer.

THINK ABOUT IT

Some people thought television would never take off. They said people would not be able to sit through a whole show. Why do you think they thought this?

6

The Internet Connects Everything

The internet is a huge network. It lets computers all over the world connect. It can use wires. It can be wireless. It can connect to TV sets and cell phones. It can connect to cars, watches, and refrigerators. People use it to share writing, pictures, and movies. They use it to play games, shop online, and make video calls. Billions of computers and other devices are connected through the internet.

Some people confuse the internet with the World Wide Web. The World Wide Web was invented in 1989 in Switzerland. It was invented by scientists who wanted to share information. The web is only part of the internet. It refers to the websites you can reach on the internet. A website is a collection of pages. The pages are about one topic. A company or school might create a website. Users visit websites by typing the addresses in a browser. Some popular browsers are Google Chrome, Firefox, Internet Explorer, and Safari. The first websites were created in the early 1990s. Some popular websites are YouTube, Twitter, Facebook, and Amazon.

Some things that happen on the internet do not use the web. Email messages travel over the internet, not the web.

On the internet, there are apps that help you find information. These are called search engines. The most popular search engine is Google. Surfing is a word that means searching on the internet. Users can surf for information. They can also surf for interesting facts or for websites.

1.28 billion
Number of websites on the internet in late 2017.

- The internet connects people all over the world.
- The World Wide Web is part of the internet.
- Websites are pages about one topic or organization.
- People use search engines to surf the internet.

The first-ever web page went live on August 6, 1991.

World Wide Web

The WorldWideWeb (W3) is a wide-area hypermedia information retrieval initiative aiming

Everything there is online about W3 is linked directly or indirectly to this document, includ

What's out there?
    Pointers to the world's online information, subjects , W3 servers, etc.
Help
    on the browser you are using
Software Products
    A list of W3 project components and their current state. (e.g. Line Mode ,X11 Viola
Technical
    Details of protocols, formats, program internals etc
Bibliography
    Paper documentation on W3 and references.
People
    A list of some people involved in the project.
History
    A summary of the history of the project.

Software Makes Everyone a Publisher

Personal computers (PCs) became available in the 1970s. This led to many changes in communication. One of the biggest was the introduction of desktop publishing. The first desktop publishing software came out in 1985. It was called PageMaker.

In the 1400s, the printing press changed how books were made. Books could be printed more quickly and cheaply than ever before. Millions of people could get books. The next big change was in the 1980s. Desktop publishing was even faster and cheaper. Books could now reach billions of people in an instant.

The Apple Macintosh was one computer that helped people think of their PC as a desktop. The computer could be used to write, store, and print documents. Word processing software made this possible. Big publishing houses used word processing software. So did smaller companies. Even individuals used it. People could create work that looked very professional. The most widely used word processing software was Microsoft Word. Online software was developed that allowed authors to publish their own books.

An Apple Macintosh desktop computer from 1984.

Desktop publishing wasn't just about documents and books. People made their own websites. They posted blogs on the web. Better software improved the look of their work. Writers could match the quality of high-tech printing presses. The internet made it easy to share this work with the whole world.

440 million
Estimated number of blogs in the world as of 2017.

- Personal computers made desktop publishing possible.
- People can use their PCs to create books.
- The software to do this is called word processing.
- Now anyone can make printed material that looks professional.

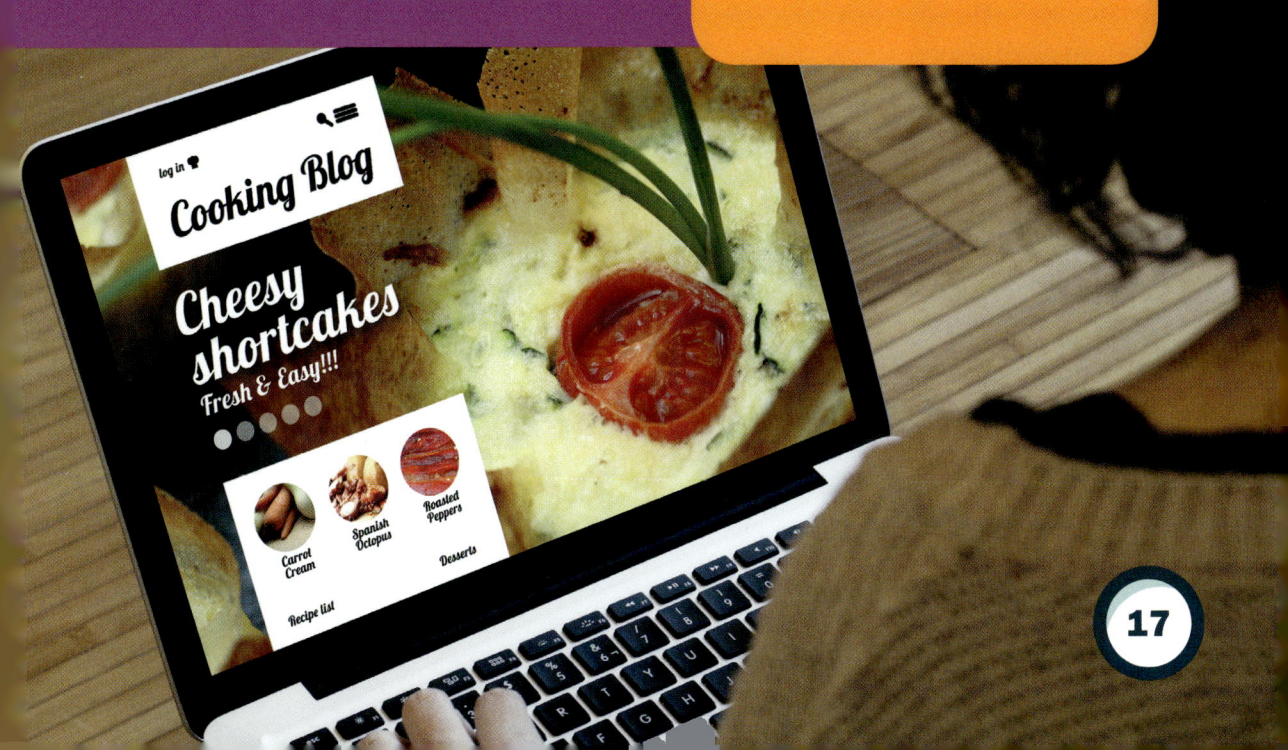

THINK ABOUT IT

Many people thought personal computers and desktop publishing would reduce our need for paper. But paper usage worldwide has increased. Why do you think this is?

8

Cell Phones Let People Talk to Anyone, Anywhere

By the 1970s, Americans were dependent on telephones. But they wanted more. They wanted their phones to be portable, so they could make calls from their cars.

The first handheld mobile phone was made by Motorola. Company employee Martin Cooper made the first mobile phone call on April 3, 1973. Early mobile phones were called car phones. They weighed about two pounds (1 kg) and were 13 inches (33 cm) long. Each one had a long antenna and 20 large buttons. It had 30 minutes of battery life. These new phones were a huge success. There were long waiting lists to get one.

Mobile or cell phones work like two-way radios. The caller's voice is changed into electrical signals. The signals are sent to the nearest cell tower. That cell tower sends the signals to the tower closest to the person being called. Then the signals are sent to the receiver's phone. The phone changes the signals back into the caller's voice.

Inventor Martin Cooper with one of the first mobile phones.

Almost all mobile phones use a cellular network. The land is divided into hexagonal cells. Each cell has its own tower. A caller can drive or walk along. The caller's phone switches from tower to tower. As long as the caller is within range of a tower, a call can be made.

By the 1990s, personal cell phones were cheap. Car phones stopped being popular. The Apple iPhone came out in 2007. It was a big hit. In 2012, Apple sold 340,000 iPhones every day.

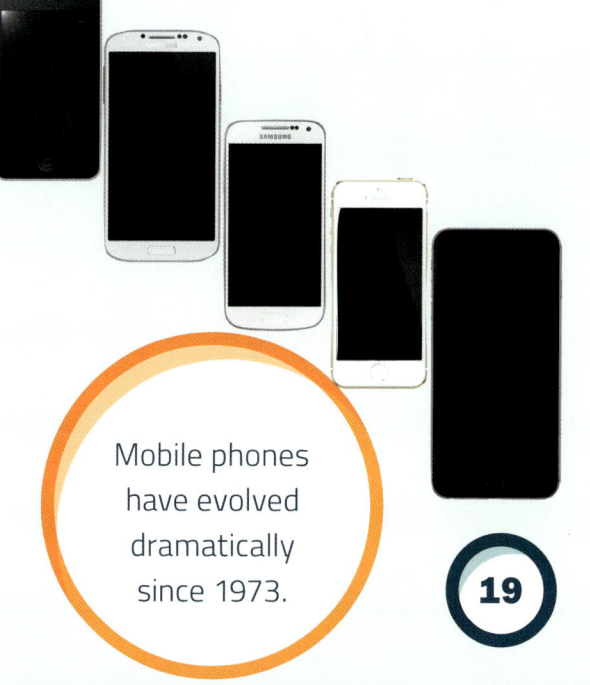

$4,000
Price of a mobile phone in 1983.

- Consumers wanted car phones.
- Early cell phones were large and heavy.
- Cell phones work like two-way radios.
- Cell phones use towers arranged in a hexagonal network.

Mobile phones have evolved dramatically since 1973.

19

9

Email and IMing Speed Up Communication

Email is short for electronic mail. Email messages are sent electronically from one computer to another. They are sent over the internet. They can be words or images. They can be documents or movies. They can be sent from one person to another. Or they can be sent to a million people all at once.

The first email was sent in 1971. Email quickly became very popular. It was easy and fast. Messages could arrive moments after they were sent. By 1996, more email was being sent than postal mail. But soon people felt email was too slow. Answers didn't come back quickly enough. They didn't want to wait for other people to open their emails. They wanted an instant response.

3.7 billion
Estimated number of email users in the world in 2017.

- Email messages are sent between computers over the internet.
- Email quickly became popular.
- Email can include pictures and movies.
- Instant messaging is faster than email.

INSTANT MESSAGING APPS

Different applications work for different types of instant messaging. New apps are appearing all the time. Some popular ones are Instagram, Snapchat, and WhatsApp. These are social networking apps. They are used for sharing photos and videos. Skype is an app for making audio and video phone calls. Google Hangouts can make group video chats.

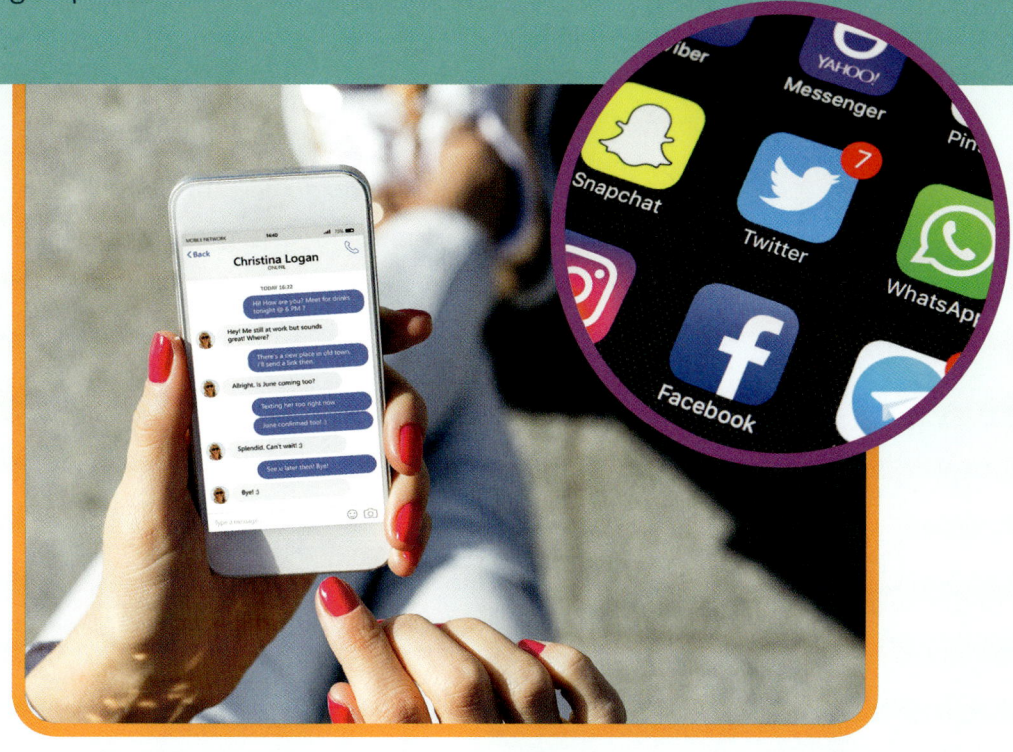

Instant messaging took off in the 1990s. IMing is sending messages in real time. People would go online. They looked to see if any friends are online. Then they texted their friends. Messages went back and forth instantly. Users could also voice chat and video chat. People under 30 are much more likely to use email and IMing than older people.

10

Web Browsers Are Gateways to the Internet

A web browser is an app. It lets people surf the web to look for websites. The browser loads the websites onto the user's computer. Website pages are created with machine code. The browser translates the code. Then people can read the pages. Some popular browsers are Chrome, Internet Explorer, Safari, and Firefox.

The first web browser was built in 1991. Early websites just had text. Mosaic was the first browser that could show text and pictures. Browsers have gotten better and better. Today's websites are highly interactive. That means the user can enter data. Browsers also remember personal settings. A user can leave a site and return later. The browser will remember the user's information.

Browsers don't all work the same way. Different browsers show websites in slightly different ways. Some websites will not work at all in some browsers. Users must be careful to use the right browser. Browsing is a popular activity. Over two trillion web searches are done every year.

HTML stands for Hypertext Markup Language, a coding language used for creating web pages and web applications.

100
Approximate number of web browsers in the world.

- Web browsers help users find websites.
- Web browsers translate machine code into words.
- Today's browsers are highly interactive.
- Websites often work differently on different browsers.

SEARCH ENGINES

Browsers contain search engines. Search engines look at the content of many websites. They put that information into databases. A user enters a search term into a search engine. They get a list of all websites that contain that term. Some popular search engines are Google, Bing, and Yahoo. Many search engines today can understand human speech.

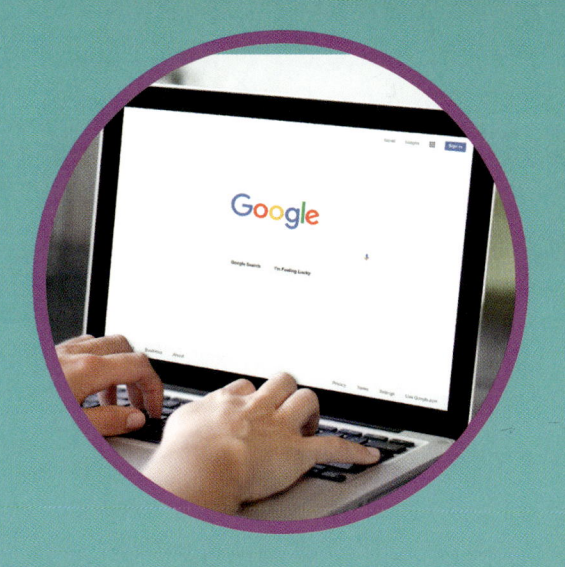

11
Social Networking Helps People Stay Connected

THINK ABOUT IT

Social networking can lead to cyberbullying. It also leads to a loss of privacy. How can these be harmful to users? What can be done about them?

Social networking is when people use websites to communicate. People use social networking to make business contacts. They use it to find others with similar interests. They use it to get news updates. Some people use these sites to promote their business.

Many people like to create a list of friends. Then they keep their friends updated all at once. There are many social networking sites. The first one was launched in 1994. It was called Geocities. Some popular sites today are Facebook, Twitter, Instagram, Tumblr, and Snapchat.

Social media refers to the content of a social networking site. Social media can take many forms. Users can share text, photos, and videos. They can post blogs and podcasts. A blog is a journal written by a person or group of people. It is updated regularly for others to read. A podcast is like a blog, except it is audio. People can subscribe to podcasts. They download them each week. Then they can listen to them whenever they want.

The first social media site, called Six Degrees, was created in 1997. Social networking is very popular. It connects people no matter where they are.

119
Number of countries where Facebook was the most popular social network in 2017.

- Social networking is a popular way to connect with friends.
- It's an easy way to keep many people up to date all at once.
- It connects businesses and people with similar interests.
- Social media is the material uploaded onto social networking sites.

12

Smartphones Put the World in Our Hands

By the end of the 1990s, many people had cell phones. Many people also had Personal Digital Assistants. PDAs were handheld devices. They could send email and search the internet. Consumers wanted one device that did both. Then the smartphone was invented. The world's first smartphone was called Simon. It was made by IBM.

IBM's Simon smartphone became available for consumers to purchase in August 1994.

A smartphone is a handheld computer. But it is a computer that can also make phone calls. Smartphones carry thousands of apps. These apps can be games, maps, or web browsers. They can be word processors, music players, and many more. The Apple iPhone

2.87 billion

Expected number of smartphone users worldwide by 2020.

- Smartphones are handheld computers that make phone calls.
- Smartphones carry thousands of apps.
- Two popular smartphones are the iPhone and the Android.
- Tablets are larger than smartphones but smaller than laptops.

26

PERSONAL ASSISTANTS

Changes in technology happen so fast. One new technology is artificial intelligence. AI is used to create personal assistants. Personal assistants are programs that respond to the human voice. A user doesn't type a request for information. The user speaks. The personal assistant provides the answers. It might respond with a voice or bring up a website. Some examples of personal assistants are Amazon's Alexa, Apple's Siri, Microsoft's Cortana, and Google Assistant.

came out in 2007. The iPhone had a touch screen and a virtual keyboard. Microsoft introduced the Android phone in 2008.

Another invention that appeared around the same time was the tablet. Tablets are smaller and cheaper than computers. But they are larger than smartphones. The larger screen makes them better for some things. People like them for reading, watching videos, and editing photos. One of the most popular tablets is the Apple iPad.

Fact Sheet

- The printing press led to many advances in science. When books were copied by hand, mistakes were made. New information spread slowly. With printed books, scientists could work from the same texts. The information they used was more reliable. Progress in science and other fields began to move ahead faster.

- The Pony Express existed from 1860 to 1861. Riders on horseback delivered mail from midwestern states to California. The riders changed horses every 10–15 miles (16–24 km). The 2,000-mile (3,200-km) trip could be made in 10 days. The Pony Express was a good idea for its time, but it was soon replaced by the telegraph.

- Frank Conrad is known as the Father of Radio Broadcasting. In the late 1940s, he broadcast from his garage. Twice each week, he played records on a phonograph. He built an audience. He introduced the idea of regular radio broadcasts. He was the first to advertise on radio.

- In 1968, the first 911 call was made. This nationwide number is for reporting emergencies. It began because of a case in New York. Someone was attacked and there was no fast way to contact police. The number 911 was chosen because it was short and easy to remember.

- The internet is powerful. But it can be interrupted. Two ways to do this are with spam and viruses. Spam is junk email. It tricks users into giving up personal information. A computer virus is malware, which is short for malicious software. It uses the internet to attack a computer. It can actually take over a computer.

- Social media can have negative effects on users. These effects include isolation, jealousy, and depression. Researchers have studied people who use social media a lot. They discovered that these people can be sad more often than happy. They can become addicted to social media. They stop seeing real friends.

Glossary

app
Short for application. A small program downloaded and generally used on mobile devices.

artificial intelligence (AI)
The development of computer systems to simulate human behavior or do things normally associated with human intelligence.

blog
Short for weblog, a regularly updated website usually produced by one person.

browser
An app that lets people surf the web to look for websites.

cyberbullying
The use of social networking or other electronic communication to intimidate, threaten, or bully someone.

database
A collection of information in a computer organized so it can be easily accessed and updated.

interactive
A two-way flow of information between a computer and a user. For example, ordering online.

literacy
The ability to read and write. Computer literacy is the ability to use computers and software.

online
Connected to or controlled by a computer.

patent
Legal ownership of an invention or the idea for an invention.

phonograph
A device that reproduced sound recorded on cylinders or records. Later called a record player.

podcast
An audio file, usually part of a series, that is downloaded onto a computer or mobile device and listened to. Subscribers generally receive regular installments.

rotary dial
A disk on the front of old telephones with finger holes and numbers that was rotated to make phone calls.

For More Information

Books

Amstutz, Lisa J. *Smartphones*. How It Works. Mendota Heights, MN: North Star Editions, 2017.

Chambers, Catherine. *The First Telephone.* DK Adventures. London: Dorling Kindersley, 2015.

Rooney, Ann. *You Wouldn't Want to Live Without the Internet*. London: Franklin Watts, 2015.

Winquist, Gloria, and Matt McCarthy. *Coding iPhone Apps for Kids: A Playful Introduction to Swift.* San Francisco: No Starch Press, 2017.

Visit 12StoryLibrary.com

Scan the code or use your school's login at 12StoryLibrary.com for recent updates about this topic and a full digital version of this book. Enjoy free access to:

- Digital ebook
- Breaking news updates
- Live content feeds
- Videos, interactive maps, and graphics
- Additional web resources

Note to educators: Visit 12StoryLibrary.com/register to sign up for free premium website access. Enjoy live content plus a full digital version of every 12-Story Library book you own for every student at your school.

Index

app, 15, 21, 26, 30, 31
artificial intelligence, 27, 30

Bell, Alexander Graham, 8-9

browser, 14, 22-23, 26, 30

cell phone, 14, 18-19, 26
computer, 14, 16-17, 20, 22, 26-27, 29, 30
Conrad, Frank, 28
Cooper, Martin, 18

email, 14, 20-21, 26, 29

Facebook, 14, 24

Gray, Elisha, 8
Gutenberg, Johannes, 6-7

Henry, Joseph, 6

internet, 14-15, 17, 20, 22, 26, 29, 31

Marconi, Guglielmo, 10
Morse, Samuel F. B., 7
Morse code, 7, 10
Motorola, 18

printing press, 6, 7, 16, 17, 28

radio, 10-11, 12-13, 18-19, 28

smartphone, 26-27, 31
social media, 24-25, 29
software, 16-17, 29

telegraph, 6-7, 8, 10, 28
telephone, 8-9, 18, 30, 31
television, 12-13

website, 14-15, 17, 22-23, 24, 27, 30

About the Author
Vicki C. Hayes has worked at WNET-TV in New York and at ABC Radio News in Washington. She has a master's degree in Film and Electronic Media and currently works as a teacher and writer.

READ MORE FROM 12-STORY LIBRARY

Every 12-Story Library Book is available in many fomats. For more information, visit 12StoryLibrary.com